PATRICIA POLACCO

BABUSHKA
Baba Yaga

SCHOLASTIC INC.
New York   Toronto   London   Auckland   Sydney
Mexico City   New Delhi   Hong Kong

ISBN 0-590-06197-6

12 11 10 9 8 7 6 5 4   1/0
                                                 14
Printed in the U.S.A.

The text is set in Sabon.
Book design by Colleen Flis.

*To the fifty American school children who went to
art camp with me in Russia in the summer of 1989.
With love to all of you,
and especially to Derek Hiashi.*

She was the last of her kind. A creature of legends. A being of the forest. She ruled her woods alone. She ate alone and slept alone, her loneliness made more bitter by the stories that were told of her—stories of the terrible, horrible Baba Yaga.

And so she watched sadly from afar as the people of the nearby village celebrated the seasons of their lives together, kept holidays together and rejoiced at weddings.

Most of all they pleasured in the birth of their young. How her arms ached just to hold a little one, if only for a moment. How she longed to have a young one of her own. But she was old now and knew that it would never be.

Many mornings the babushkas bustled by her forest with their grandchildren.

"I wish I had a grandchild," she would say to herself. Then one day, as she came close to the dacha of one of the babushkas, she saw some of her clothes drying on the clothesline.

"I shall borrow these," thought Baba Yaga. "I will be a babushka instead of a Baba Yaga."

She looked at the reflection of herself in the stream. "I shall have to scrub the forest off from my skin, cut my nails, comb my hair…but my ears," she said with a sigh, "what will I do about my ears?"

Then she remembered that babushkas always wore scarves.

She carefully dressed herself. "Yes," she said with glee. "I look just like a babushka!"

She bade the creatures of the forest a fond goodbye. "I'm going into the village." She beamed.

As she entered the village she was warmly greeted by the other babushkas sitting under the shade of the tree in the center of the square.

"Come, sister…sit with us," one of them said.

Baba Yaga smiled inside; no one recognized her.

They showed her a brand-new baby that had been born just that morning.

"This is my new grandchild," one proud babushka chirped.

"And this is my Masha. Isn't she dear?"

One after another the babushkas shared their babies with her.

Just then, Natasha and her little son, Victor, passed by them.

One of the babushkas whispered, "Too bad, that little one has no babushka to care for him while his mother works."

As they went on admiring the other babies, Baba Yaga walked right after Natasha and Victor. She followed them down the road and into their little house.

"Old one," Natasha greeted her cheerfully, "how is it that you are here?"

"Perhaps you can help me," Baba Yaga said. "I am new in the village and quite alone. I need a place to stay. I can cook, clean and take care of your son for you."

"I have no money to pay you," Natasha answered sadly.

"I need no money. All I will need is a place to rest my old head and perhaps a little food."

"Then you shall, indeed, stay with us, old one."

"I kiss your eyes and I hold you in my heart!" Baba Yaga said happily. And stay she did.

Oh, how happy she was! When Natasha went to work in the mornings, she and Victor cleaned the little house together. When all of the tasks were done, Baba Yaga took Victor to the edge of the woods. This was her favorite part of the day.

She pulled Victor into her lap. As she cradled him there, she told him wondrous tales and legends of the great forest. She sang him songs that he had never heard before. Then they would just sit there together and daydream without words at all.

As time passed, their love for each other grew and grew. Baba Yaga took as much pride in Victor's life as a real grandmother would. She was well loved in return. And she had earned her place with all of the other grandmothers under the shade tree in the village square.

Baba Yaga was happy and content with her new life.

Then one day, as the babushkas gathered, they started telling stories to the children.

One spoke of "Ivan Tsarevich, the gray wolf and the firebird." Another told the tale of "Sister Alyonushka and Brother Ivanushka." They all laughed.

Then one of them rose from her seat, her eyes narrowed and her voice hissed as she unfolded the legend of the horrible, wicked Baba Yaga!

"She eats babies," the woman said as all stared in wide-eyed amazement. "She flies through the air on an old stump and casts spells."

"She comes out of the forest and takes children in the dead of night," another warned.

"She is ugly…a hag…evil and hateful!" yet another sang out.

"And if you don't behave, she'll come and get *you*!" one said to Victor as he hugged close to Baba Yaga.

That night when she put Victor to bed, he cried himself to sleep. Baba Yaga tried to calm him, but her own heart was heavy and sad. There was only one thing to do: go back to her home in the forest before Victor learned who she really was.

She left a note for Victor and his mother saying, "I kiss your eyes and hold you in my heart, my beloved ones. I will never forget your kindness." Signed, "Your babushka."

She left, never to return.

For a very long time Victor went to the edge of the forest almost every day. It helped him remember his babushka, whom he missed so.

Then one day, as he sat, he saw yellow, evil eyes peering at him from the deep blackness of the forest. When he could make out the shapes that went with the evil burning eyes, he saw that the eyes belonged to a pack of wolves.

He screamed for help, but he was soon surrounded by them.

The villagers came running, but the wolves snapped at them and snarled when the villagers tried to get close to Victor.

"Oh, please," his mother cried…"Someone help my baby!"

At that very moment the trees parted and out of the forest crashed a fearsome figure, snarling and gnashing its teeth at the wolves.

"The Baba Yaga!" the crowd screamed.

The creature eyed them menacingly as it sprang like a cat at the savage wolves.

The wolves scattered and ran.

Then the creature moved closer to the child, who was howling with fright. When the gnarled hands reached for the boy, his mother screamed.

A voice from the crowd said, "The Baba Yaga is going to eat him!"

As the creature snatched the child from the ground, the villagers gasped with horror.

With a loud smack, it kissed the child, then smiled through eyes brimming with tears. The weathered arms held the boy close and rocked him so gently.

Although she didn't look the same, Victor knew that warm hug well.

"Babushka!" Victor cried, and he hugged her back.

There was a great celebration in the village that night for a very unusual babushka! There were flowers given. Bread and salt offered. Songs sung and dances danced.

One of the babushkas moved close to her and took Baba Yaga's hands and called out, "Those who judge one another on what they hear or see, and not on what they know of them in their hearts, are fools indeed!"

"Hear, hear!" the mayor sang out as everyone cheered.

Baba Yaga smiled and accepted, with grace, their tributes. For the rest of her days she kissed many eyes and held scores of hearts in her good keeping. She was spoken of in the highest regard and well loved.

From that time on, she was known as Babushka Baba Yaga!